T0247169

The
Franchise

THE OPPORTUNITY

The
Franchise

PATRICK JONES
with BRENT CHARTIER

darbycreek
MINNEAPOLIS

Text copyright © 2013 by Lerner Publishing Group, Inc.

Darby Creek
A division of Lerner Publishing Group, Inc.
241 First Avenue North
Minneapolis, MN 55401 U.S.A.

Website address: www.lernerbooks.com

Cover and interior photographs © Rubberball/Getty Images (boy);
© iStockphoto.com/Ermin Gutenberger (lights); © iStockphoto.com/Jordan
McCullough (title texture).

Main body text set in Janson Text LT Std 12/17.
Typeface provided by Linotype AG.

The Cataloging-in-Publication Data for *The Franchise* is on file at the Library
of Congress.
    ISBN: 978-1-4677-1375-7 (LB)
    ISBN: 978-1-4677-1675-8 (EB)

Manufactured in the United States of America
1 – SB – 7/15/13

In order to succeed, your desire for success should be greater than your fear of failure.

—Bill Cosby

PROLOGUE

Dear Mr. Latrell Baker:

Congratulations, you've made an impression. And earned an opportunity. You will be an intern working for the general manager of my newly acquired Los Angeles Stars NFL team.

I was impressed with your award-winning science project—an algorithm to predict the best possible defensive positioning based on the most likely offensive play. My other businesses succeed because they make decisions based on measurable factors. But too often in the realm of sports, judgments seem to be made on instinct and biased experience. I expect you to bring to this opportunity your enthusiasm and passion for evidence-based decision making.

As with all my interns, your story reminds me of my own years growing up in DC. I was raised by a single mother who made me study because she knew education was the only path out of poverty. I loved football, but I was physically unable to compete. Like you, I knew that no amount of hard work or passion would pay off unless I excelled when given an opportunity to prove myself. This, Latrell, is that opportunity!

Sincerely,
Harmon Holt

ONE

August 5 (Sunday)

"How do you like your room, Latrell?" A thin white guy with short black hair stood outside my door.

I nodded. "Latrell Baker, from DC. How'd you know my name?"

He laughed—giggled, really—and pointed at my mirror, where I had taped a sign with my name on it. It was the sign the limo driver was holding when he met me at the airport.

"Kevin Whitney." The guy stuck his hand out. His nails were bitten down to the quick.

I shook his hand, which is always awkward with a white guy. "I think we're the only two in the dorm," I said. "Are you a Holt intern too?"

He walked past me. "No, what's that?" he asked as he gazed at a poster I'd hung on the wall of the Baltimore Ravens' last Super Bowl team.

It was a dumb question on my part. The scholarship only went to kids from Carver High, and there were no white guys at Carver High anymore. I told him about the internship.

"Sounds cool," he said. "I'm interning with a defense contractor, researching materials to protect soldiers in combat."

I felt stupid. He was doing good work, while I was calling pass rushes.

I was about to ask Kevin more about the dorm when my phone rang. I looked at it. It said *Bob Milliken*. The L.A. Stars' general manager was calling me. My hand shook; I hoped Kevin didn't notice.

"It's my boss." Kevin nodded, shot me a thumbs-up, and walked away.

I took a deep breath and answered the call.

"Hello, Mr. Milliken."

"Hello, Latrell. I'm downstairs. Mind if I come up?" Milliken and I had sent a number of e-mails back and forth. This was the first time we'd talked on the phone. But I knew his voice from the TV interviews he'd given while he was GM of the Ravens. They won two Super Bowls while he was running the team. Sometimes his face was on TV more than any of his star players.

"No, it'd be great to meet you." What a stupid answer. Would everything I said be a fumble?

"Great. Fire up your computer. I want to see this famous system of yours."

"Sure thing." Of course, my computer was already on. It was always on. I was always working on the system. Plus, I needed to enter data for new players.

Mr. Milliken knocked on my door. I opened it and started to speak, but stopped when I saw he was talking on his cell phone. I sat back down at my computer and waited.

And waited. And waited.

"Sorry, kid. Busy time of year, but you'll learn that soon enough." He stuck out his hand. It was big and heavy, weighed down by two Super Bowl rings. When he shook my hand, I felt as though he'd swallowed it. "So, tell me more about this system."

"It's only ever been tried in high school game conditions, but—" I stopped talking when he took another call. After a few minutes, he turned his attention back to me. "So, like I was saying—"

He cut me off and pointed to the poster on my wall. "That was a great team. We had everything. Great defense, great special teams, and we played as a family. All for one."

"And the Terrible Two!" I pointed at the two large men in the back of the team photo: the outside linebackers, "Smackdown" Joe Schultz and Frank "The Franchise" Foley. Schultz was now the Stars' defensive coordinator. Foley was the linebacker coach. I looked forward to meeting them. I'd grown up a Ravens fan, and they were my heroes.

"With the Stars," Milliken said, "I've assembled the best players in the league."

I stared at the floor. I had last year's stats in a data set. He couldn't be more wrong, but I kept quiet. Though I'd never had a job, I knew you didn't correct your boss on day one.

"Now, show me your system."

He stood over my shoulder as I talked. I probably gave too much detail, because that's how I get when I get talking about math stuff, totally obsessed. I talked while he listened. At least I thought he was listening. When I glanced over my shoulder at him, his eyes were riveted on his phone, not me or my computer. I felt like an incomplete pass.

* * *

I'd gotten lucky at Carver. The high school defensive coordinator was the stats teacher. It hadn't taken me more than five minutes to make him understand my algorithm. And once we got results, the rest of the coaching staff followed our lead. One state championship later, there were a whole lot of football jerseys in stats class.

I had a sense Milliken wouldn't be so easy.

TWO

August 9 (Thursday)

Today was my first trip to Stars Stadium, one of the newest and biggest stadiums in the league, and my chance to meet the Stars' players and coaching staff as they practiced for their pre-season opener.

A limo pulled up to the dorm to take me to the stadium. "I don't drive many kids around," said the driver. He reminded me of my Uncle Randall. "You must be pretty special."

"Just lucky, I guess," I said. I learned long ago you shouldn't brag on yourself.

When we got to the stadium, we drove up to the players' entrance. Guards stood by the gates while shiny new Mercedes, Hummers, and Caddies sat in the players' parking lot.

The limo driver turned to me. "Even when I drive kids, I don't drive any here. You *are* special." I fingered the L.A. Stars staff badge that hung around my neck like a gold chain.

I smiled. "I guess you're right."

From the limo, I walked past a guard shack into the main building. There was a long hallway lined with action shots—the biggest hits and biggest plays in the team's short two-year history.

At the other end of the hallway, a huge man walked toward me with his head down. He seemed to be looking for something on the ground.

I pressed against the hallway wall to avoid him.

It didn't work. When he got close, he spoke. "Have you seen a pair of sunglasses anywhere?"

"Sunglasses?" I asked. I could see the back of one of those sunglasses straps on the front of his huge neck.

"Yeah, white Ray-Bans." He gestured with hands that were bigger than my face.

"On a purple strap?" I asked.

"Yes!" he shouted like a kid on Christmas morning. "Have you seen 'em?"

I reached behind him and pulled his glasses over his shoulder.

"Well, I'll be. Thank you, kid," said the man. He walked toward a door marked Weight Room while I continued down the hallway toward the light and the stadium field.

I took a few steps onto the turf. The stadium was even bigger than I'd imagined, making me feel even smaller. Guys were lined up on the field, doing drills. There was lots of yelling, but none by the head coach, Chad Allen. He spoke to a TV reporter while assistant coaches ran the drills. Near me, players pushed huge training sleds as if they were pillows. I stood in awe as the sounds of hits and slams echoed in the empty stadium, reminding me that football wasn't a contact sport, but a collision one.

"Stand there too long and you'll get hit." I turned so fast, I felt dizzy. It was Milliken.

He put a hand on my shoulder while the other clutched his phone. "Why aren't you suited up?"

"Suited up? Me?" I swallowed hard at the same time I heard a big crack-on-crack of helmets crashing together like cars on the interstate.

Milliken looked at a group of men on the sidelines, each one holding a clipboard. "Hey, Schultz!" he called out. One of the men looked over. "You said Latrell was gonna play today? I know Earle got him a jersey. He's ready when you are."

"But I—" my heart beat fast in my chest.

Milliken turned to me. "No, I insist. It's the best way to learn the game, get your hands dirty."

Smackdown Schultz walked over. Like the guy in the stadium hallway looking for his Ray-Bans, he towered over me. A five-time Pro Bowl linebacker, he'd gone into coaching after a knee injury cut his career short. He inspected me like Mom did chicken at the grocery store. "Ready to play, kid? Where's your uniform?"

I tried to speak, but nothing came out. This was not what I expected. Not at all.

Then Milliken slammed his meaty paw on my shoulder so hard, I wished I was wearing pads. "He's just busting you, Latrell. Welcome to the Stars. This is defensive coordinator Joe Schultz—"

As he said that, a man emerged from the tunnel and shouted, "Roxanne!" We all turned.

"And that," said Milliken, "is none other than Franchise Foley himself."

"You're kidding me. *That's* Frank Foley?" I asked.

"The one and only," said Schultz.

When he heard his name, Frank walked toward us. He reached up, tipped the glasses now perched on his huge head, and looked at me as he did so. "Hey, it's my sunglasses-finder."

THREE

August 10 (Friday) First Preseason Game

"Fine 'em a thousand dollars!" Milliken shouted into his phone. He only shouted when something went wrong on the field. The way things had been going, his throat must be hurting. In the fourth quarter, the Stars were behind by forty. "Plays like that won't put butts in these seats or dollars in the bank."

While he yelled, I helped myself to another soda. The GM's box at Stars Stadium was full of food, drinks, and plenty of Milliken's rich friends. I listened in on their conversations.

Milliken's friends didn't seem to know a thing about football.

"Why's your nose buried in that computer, kid?" asked a guy with silver hair, fake orange skin, and gold cufflinks. "The game's out there on the field."

I started to explain my system, but like Milliken before, a few minutes into my talk, his eyes glazed over. Was I that boring, or were the drinks the bartender poured that strong?

Milliken walked over. "Latrell's my intern," he said. I didn't like how strongly he said the word *my*.

"An intern. I gotta get me one of them," Cufflink said, then snorted a laugh.

"I'm letting him off easy this week, but next week, he's going to learn the hardest part of the job." Milliken put his hand on my shoulder.

"Hardest part?" I asked.

"On the weekend, football is a game. But during the week, it's something else."

"What's that?"

Milliken smiled, but it seemed as fake as Cufflink's tanned face. "A business."

"Latrell, what's up? The Stars lost, and I had serious money on 'em," Uncle Randall said. I pictured him sitting on the couch in the tiny row house I shared with him, my mom, and my grandma back in DC. I'd always give him tips on what teams to bet on; he usually won.

"You shouldn't bet in the preseason anyway," I said.

"But I thought with you there, they'd be—"

"I'm not sure if this whole internship thing is going to work out." I spoke softly, even though the words weighed on me as I rode alone in the limo back to my dorm room.

"Just a second," Randall said. "Your mom wants the phone."

"Hello, son." Mom's voice was soft and firm. I could picture her big smile.

"Mom, how do I get them to listen to me?" I asked.

There was a long pause on the other end.

"I guess do the same thing you did at school: study. Study the men around you. Find out what matters to them."

For having just a GED, Mom could be pretty smart about stuff. Only problem was, the things people like Milliken cared about were exactly the things I didn't have: money, power, status, or experience.

"What matters to them is winning," I said.

"Then show them that if they would've listened to you, they would've won," Mom said.

The three of us continued to talk long into the night. I wanted to hear the regular stuff—the home news. The connection meant everything.

I finally turned off the light and hung up the phone around 2 a.m. But I'd no more shut my eyes than my phone rang.

When I picked up the phone, it was a man's voice. "Hey, how's it going?" His words were slurred and heavy. "Have you seen my sunglasses?"

FOUR

August 16 (Thursday a.m.)

It was Franchise Foley himself, but I was too groggy from lack of sleep to be excited, even if the call was from a future Hall of Famer.

"I'm just kidding about the glasses," he said, laughing. "Hey, Milliken told me to look at that computer thing of yours to help with defense. You doing anything right now?"

I looked at my phone. The time read 2:14. "Mr. Foley, it's the middle of the night."

"Is it really?" He seemed shocked by the news. "Sorry. I don't sleep like I used to."

"Can it wait until tomorrow?" I asked.

"Sure. Roxanne and me—Frank, no more of this Mr. Foley stuff—will come by at eleven. I'll fix lunch. You like Maryland Chicken?"

Any chance to have lunch with a star like Frank was an opportunity of a lifetime. And if he was willing to listen—*really* listen—to how my system worked, all the better. "Eleven sounds good," I said. "As for Maryland Chicken, you know my family's originally from Baltimore, right? That's why I'm a Ravens fan."

Frank laughed. "I thought that'd get your attention."

"By the way, who's Roxanne?" I asked. I remembered it was the name he'd yelled at the stadium the other day.

"She's my daughter," Frank said with pride in voice, "and the most beautiful girl in L.A."

* * *

Frank's daughter was a dream. She drove while Frank sat in the passenger seat, and I sat in back. It was a clunker of a car, not like the limo that took me everywhere. I tried to feel comfortable, but Roxanne being so pretty cranked up my shy dial just far enough that all I could do was sit in silence. When I learned she was a senior in high school, I wanted to cheer.

"First, we'll eat. Then, you show me the thing on the computer," Frank said as the car turned through streets in an older neighborhood. "Later, Roxanne can show you more of the town."

Roxanne glanced at me through the rear-view mirror. "I'd like that."

When we pulled up to the house, I was shocked that it looked like the homes in my old neighborhood, not some big mansion fit for a guy who'd won two Super Bowls.

Roxanne went inside while I followed Frank to the backyard. "I learned to make Maryland Chicken from a guy who was a seven-year Pro Bowler. Seeing as I made it to the Pro Bowl only six times, it wasn't my place to doubt him," said Frank. He lifted the lid on the grill to show two chickens, each cut in half, browning over coals.

"I wouldn't doubt him, either," I laughed.

Frank put the lid down. "Now, show me your system."

I set my laptop up on a table on the back porch while Roxanne brought out drinks. I pretended to look into my computer while it booted up, but I watched her instead. Although she was about my height, her long neck made her seem taller. She didn't say much and seemed relieved that Frank and I were so busy reviewing my system.

When it was time to eat, her expression changed. Frank went to take the chicken off the grill, but forgot where he put the tongs. Roxanne hunted them down and brought them to him. Then Frank burned his hand on the grill lid, not too badly, but enough for Roxanne to put ice in a towel for him. He had questions for me, but I had one I wanted to ask Roxanne, but couldn't.

What was wrong with Frank?

FIVE

"But why give a higher score to a guy who sacks a quarterback based on the number of defensive backs?" asked Frank while I punched in numbers.

"If I've got fewer men on the defensive line, then the guy who sacks the QB is golden. It's all about strategy based on probability."

I typed away. A moment later, I hit the enter key. "A sack with two defensive backs, in the current season, the odds are 1 in 40. With three defensive backs, 1 in 180, and throw in another

D-back, now we're talking 1 in 320. That's why he gets a higher score in my system. I'll bet he sacks more QBs than BK does fries any given Sunday."

Frank laughed, but I didn't join in. I was too tired. It was almost five o'clock. We'd been at it more than four hours, but Frank looked as though he could go on like this for days.

Roxanne joined us on the porch, carrying a small box. It wasn't leftovers, because there weren't any: Frank and I had done serious damage to the chicken. "Dad, why did you order more?"

When Frank saw the box, he sprinted toward it like a loose ball. He reached for it, but she held on, staring him down. Frank wrenched it from her hands.

"Waynan, you never let me down!" shouted Frank, smiling as he held the box.

"Dad, you know how much I hate this," said Roxanne. Whatever was in the box obviously upset her.

Frank placed a big hand on her shoulder. "Honey, it'll be okay."

"It's not the answer." Roxanne turned her back and walked away. Before hitting the door, she yelled over her shoulder. "Latrell, let's get out of here. I'll show you the town."

* * *

I don't know why, but whatever happened on the porch between Roxanne and her dad kept me from being shy around her. I guess I'd figured anyone with a dad in the NFL got the smooth ride, but I was getting the sense her life was anything but.

I packed my gear and thanked Frank for the meal, and Roxanne and I took off in the clunker.

Roxanne was quiet. She drove while I surfed the radio and watched the scenery.

After a while, she drove by a beach and outdoor park packed with people. In the park, a group of people surrounded folks dressed as clowns. Some clowns juggled; one breathed fire. I had to speak up. "Man, you put a fire-breathin' clown in my neighborhood, and either the cops or the gangs would be on him so fast."

That did it. Roxanne laughed so hard, I thought she might get into an accident. She pulled into the nearest parking space so we could watch.

I didn't know where to go in the conversation, so I waited for her to speak.

But she didn't.

Instead, she cried.

I had to say something. "What's the matter? Was it the box?"

"It's not just the box, it's everything. It is so hard." She wiped her eyes and started talking really fast about her dad and his forgetfulness. "He had so many hits to the head and concussions throughout his career, the doctor says his brain is damaged." I remembered helping him find his glasses. But I'd also spent four incredible hours with him, talking about stats and my system. How damaged could it be?

"He seemed fine on the porch."

"The doctor said if something interests him, he's okay, and football's been his life." She wiped her eyes. "I drive because he always gets lost. He rarely sleeps. He has no short-term memory.

He's on good behavior now, but his mood is all over the place. I could go on."

"Then what was in the box?" I asked.

"They're pills that he says help him. He gets them from Waynan, a former player who sends them to players all over the country."

"Isn't that a good thing?" I asked.

"But the pills won't help," said Roxanne. "The brain damage is permanent."

I thought for a moment. "Maybe the team can help, the Stars. Or the Ravens. I bet if Mr. Milliken knew—"

"They know, but they don't care." Roxanne looked at me. She reached over to touch my face and smiled. "You really are just an intern."

Her long fingers lingered on my skin even as she made fun of me.

"The team is a lot like my dad," Roxanne said, now all serious.

"How's that?"

She looked away from me. "Both have no short-term memory."

SIX

August 20 (Monday)

"Latrell Baker?" I raised my hand, my black hand in the sea of white guys that was the internship class at Excaliber Academy. The teacher, Mr. Casey, a white guy with a blond soul patch and thick, wire-rim glasses, continued with announcements.

"On Mondays and Fridays, you'll normally work full-time in your internships," said Mr. Casey. "The other days, you'll attend regular classes. You'll all be in the same class, unless you're being tutored." I ducked my head. I was going to get to know the academy tutors pretty well. My grades were like the slope of a mountain: all As in math at the top, Ds in everything else at the bottom.

"Today, you'll each give a brief presentation on your internship," Mr. Casey explained. "From time to time, you'll be asked to give us an update, and in mid-October, you'll bring in someone from your work assignment to speak to the class. Everyone understand?"

Everyone nodded.

"Now, let's begin. We'll go alphabetically, starting with Rashem Albert. Mr. Albert?"

One of the few other black kids stood up. He stared at the floor, coughed, and stared down again, like he was afraid the floor would move. Rashem talked like his audience was the white tiles beneath him.

"Mr. Albert, please come to the front of the class, and speak up!" Mr. Casey said. "These are you peers. You have nothing to fear. This is a great opportunity to practice your presentation skills."

"Sorry," Rashem mumbled, then walked

slowly to the front of the class. I could tell that, like me, he felt odd wearing the uniform—blue slacks, white shirt, and red sweater.

Rashem started to talk, but I tuned him out as I thought about what I would say. Would I say how I really felt? I work for a terrible football team and for a guy who doesn't listen to me. The only guy who will listen loses the hat on his head, and I feel like a charity case. Or would I lie and say everything was fine?

"Latrell Baker." It was just like Rashem and I were in the movies, sending the two brothers out to die first.

I walked slowly to the front of the room, my hands in my pockets to hide that they were shaking.

"I'm Latrell Baker, from DC, and my internship is with the L.A. Stars football team and—"

Immediately, words like "wow," "cool," "great," and "dang" bounced around the room

"Do you get to meet the players?" someone asked.

"Do you go to practices and watch films and all that stuff?" asked another.

The questions came at me fast like a blitz.

When I sat down, I felt like I'd passed some test.

SEVEN

August 30 (Thursday) Final Preseason Game
"What was that?!!!" Schultz stomped his feet like a three-year-old throwing a tantrum. He shouted at two guys on the field who pretended not to hear him: a defensive back and safety who were supposed to guard a league-leading receiver for the Seahawks. During the play, the two had pulled right as though headed to a barbecue on the Seahawks' sideline. Meanwhile, the receiver pulled left, caught the pass, and took twenty untouched strides for a TD.

One touchdown might not mean much, but

that was number six for Seattle. All we had on the board was a field goal from the Stars' kicker, whose name I couldn't pronounce.

I'd watched the first half from the GM box, but Milliken let me watch from the sideline during the second. I stood far away from the action: hands in my pockets, laptop in my backpack, and my good ideas buried like a sacked quarterback.

After a middle linebacker, Johnson, missed a tackle, Schultz screamed at Frank. Frank stood, taking the verbal hits like he used to take the physical hits. Schultz tossed his clipboard at Frank's feet. For a second, the two former teammates stared at each other the way they once did opposing linemen.

* * *

"I started my first business in high school." Milliken stood in the middle of the locker room, which had gone graveyard quiet. He'd asked me to attend what he said would be a motivational speech to the team. It was my first time in the players' sanctuary.

I stood in back, next to Frank. His arms were crossed, and his eyes had this almost blank stare. If they'd used my system, we'd be eating cake or celebrating however teams celebrate. Instead, Milliken was chewing out the team.

"I sold that business, made enough to put me through law school. Hard work, dedication, and a vision, that's what it takes!" Milliken raised his voice, but he never really shouted. "I didn't see any of that on the field today. You're not earning your salaries. Give me one good reason I shouldn't tear up your contracts, send you to the unemployment office, and pick up fifty-three new guys for opening day!"

The room went stone silent. Head Coach Allen said nothing. Finally, Schultz walked up and took over while Milliken carried his angry stare to the locker room door. "Guys, we've got work to do and not much time left," Schultz said softly.

Then Maxwell, the offensive coordinator, rallied the troops, followed by Allen. So far in the preseason, Allen had spent most of his time talking to the press, but not to players.

I looked at Milliken. He had Frank fixed with a hard stare, which was unusual. From what I observed, everyone ignored Frank but me.

Milliken then started for the hallway, motioning me to follow. As I did, I felt nervous. The closer we got to the season, the less time he had for me. He didn't care about my system, or about me. I was dead weight. Or so I thought.

In the empty hallway, Milliken poked my chest. "You've got a new assignment: Frank. Latrell, your job is to see he doesn't embarrass us."

I shook my head slowly, trying to show I took this first real assignment seriously. "How do I do that?"

Milliken turned his back and answered his phone, but not my question.

EIGHT

September 3 (Monday)

Roxanne picked me up in the clunker. I told her I wanted to help out with the meal, but I didn't say a thing about Milliken telling me to look after her dad.

When we stopped at a store, she said they needed soda and paper plates. I spent my last ten dollars, hoping Mom would send money at the end of the week.

"Dad really likes you," Roxanne said as she drove to her house. "How many times did the two of you talk on the phone this weekend?"

"I lost count." It was pushing it, but I said it anyway. While my specialty was defense, I knew advancing the ball meant you had to take chances. "Well, I really like your dad—and his daughter."

She smiled and gave my hand a quick squeeze. It wasn't much, but given my track record with girls, it felt like I'd made ten touchdowns in row.

* * *

It was a repeat of my last trip to Frank's home. Once dinner was over, Roxanne went inside while Frank and I talked football on the back porch.

"The linebackers aren't blitzing at the right time or in the right places," I said. I'd given up explaining my system to him because he kept asking the same questions. I needed to somehow make it simpler. "It's not all Schultz's fault. Johnson's too slow to react and too—"

Frank interrupted. "Listen, don't say anything bad about Johnson. He's like a son to me."

I paused for a moment. Just the other day,

I'd heard Milliken on the phone, talking about trading Johnson. Frank saw the team as a family; Milliken saw dollar signs and bottom lines.

"If you have video from the last game, I can show you how my system works," I said.

Frank liked the idea. Not as much as me, though. I knew the only way to review plays was in the living room, the same room where Roxanne sat.

I followed Frank into the living room, then put in the DVD. Frank took a seat in a big lounge chair, leaving only the couch. I smiled before sitting down next to Roxanne.

After the opening kickoff, I paused the video while Frank reviewed the first play. "Look at their offensive line. It's obvious they're gonna rush, probably a sweep to the strong side. But we were set up for the pass play," he said.

I showed him my laptop, which predicted the same play. "The only problem with my system is that it doesn't work if the offense chooses unexpected plays—or if nobody listens."

Frank glanced at the laptop. "There's another problem. There are endless variations in defensive positioning, some so subtle that someone who never played—like yourself—couldn't imagine. It could be as simple as the position of the center's foot, and no computer knows that."

I wasn't insulted. Instead, I was intrigued. "Can you show me?"

Frank looked around for something to write on. He went to the kitchen and came back with a stack of the paper plates and a pen he used to sign autographs. He set up a TV tray and drew the play like he'd been doing it since birth. He held the plate up. "That's how everyone should have been positioned. That's a winning defense, the Franchise Foley way."

I glanced at Roxanne, and she gave me a look I'd rarely seen from her. A smile, big and beautiful. Frank's expression was different, too, not one of confusion, but of total concentration.

Within an hour, there were maybe a dozen paper plates on the floor.

Two hours later, thirty plates with amazing NFL plays were strewn about the living room.

At midnight, there were so many plates on the floor you couldn't see carpet.

It was late. Roxanne still had to drive me to the dorm.

In the clunker, she spoke. "You're good for my dad."

"Thanks," I said. "I hope so."

"That's why I like you." She squeezed my hand again. I felt a rush.

Part of me wanted to kiss her, but I thought she might shy away, thought she might play the Franchise Foley school of defense.

I thought I knew football, but Frank had taught me I still had a lot to learn. And I'd be happy to visit his house and sit on the couch with his daughter as often as he asked.

NINE

September 4 (Tuesday)

"You wanted to see me, Mr. Milliken?" I asked. He hardly ever called me to his office alone, so I figured I must have screwed up. But then I'd been given so little to do, it wasn't like there was much I *could* screw up.

"Sit down, Latrell." I did as I was told. He stood, sighed, looked at his phone. "Do you know how many kids would kill for the opportunity you've been given?"

I wanted to tell him I wasn't *given* anything, I earned it, but I let it go. "I know people in class are jealous."

"Then why did I hear that you disrespected your internship in class today?"

I shrunk in my chair. "I didn't mean anything by it. We have to give updates every once in a while, and I just told everyone I hadn't done much."

Head shake, phone look, and a sigh. "If you have a problem, you come to me. Got it?"

"Yes, sir." I let the chair swallow me. "If you give me a chance to show you my—"

"Here's what I want—" he started, but stopped as soon as his phone rang. A minute later he began again. "Your model is all about predicting the right moves based on what's happened in the past, so I have another assignment for you."

I sat up. "This game is the perfect match-up for us with their weak running attack—" I began.

I got the headshake-phone-stare-and-sigh combo platter. "Not that, Latrell. I want to you gather data from other teams, crunch the numbers, then tell me how we should respond."

"Okay, I won't let you down. But I know defense best, and with Frank's help, I could—"

"Research the concessions for each team. Find out what they charge for things like beer, hot dogs, and nachos, and then tell me what we should charge," Milliken said. "Then, find out if there's a connection between concession profits and team wins. My guess is that when teams are losing, the fans eat and drink more to distract them. Can you do this for me?"

I was in shock. I'd left my home to come to L.A. to research the price of beer and nachos. Worse, I knew he had to have marketing and sales people in the organization who already did this crap. He was giving me busywork. There were about a hundred things I wanted to scream, but only two words left my lips, the ones I knew Milliken wanted to hear. "Yes, sir."

TEN

September 9 (Sunday) Phoenix Cardinals

"They should've blitzed on second and ten against this team," I whispered, but even if I shouted, Milliken wouldn't have heard. He was carrying on three conversations, none with me. One in person with his head scout in the booth, one over the phone, and one with someone on the sidelines. And he was tweeting the game live.

Milliken pushed the scout to one side. "You watch college football, Latrell?" he asked.

"Not much." I lowered my laptop screen. One window ran defense. The other calculated the price point for fans who ordered extra jala-penos on their nachos.

"Next week, I want you to watch the Ohio State–Michigan State game. Watch it with Frank."

"I can definitely do that." Frank was an All-American from Michigan State.

"I'd like to ditch Johnson and his long-term contract, and both teams have linebackers I'd like to draft next year," he continued. It was the first time I'd had Milliken's full attention, prob-ably because of the carnage on the field behind him. Over his shoulder, I saw the score change: another six, make it seven, for the Cardinals. "Henderson here, my head scout," he said, pointing, "he likes the Buckeye kid, but I hear good things about the MSU kid."

"I don't really know how to scout or evaluate talent," I admitted.

"Skill is skill is skill." Milliken pointed at my computer. "Run the numbers. Gather all the data, and not just football stuff. Get their grades, anything you can find out."

"How about their injury history?" I asked.

"If you think that's important, but I tell

you, most kids today aren't as tough as the old-timers. You know why they gave Frank the nickname 'Franchise'? He didn't miss a game in seventeen years, not one. Most kids can't go seventeen days without needing a Band-Aid for something."

"I'll see what I can find out about injuries, especially concussions—"

Milliken snorted. "Don't bother with that. If we drafted players who never had concussions, we'd have a team of punters. Concussions are as much of part of this game as cheerleaders and tailgate parties."

I cracked my knuckles so as not to ball them into a fist and punch Milliken. I'd lose my scholarship and internship, but maybe he'd experience what a concussion fog felt like.

"So, next Saturday, before we head to Dallas, watch the MSU–Ohio game, crunch the numbers," Milliken said with a smile he seemed to switch on and off. "If I like your report, I'll let you pitch your system to Schultz."

"Thank you, Mr. Milliken. I appreciate—" was as far as I got before there was another call.

I looked at the scoreboard. The Stars were losing, which was bad, but I knew two things: I'd won another opportunity, and, from my research, beer sales would be good.

ELEVEN

September 12 (Wednesday)

"Here's your opportunity, Latrell," Milliken said as the door to his office opened. In walked Smack-down Schultz, whistle around his neck, clipboard in hand, his eyes looking through me like I was an empty space cleared by an offensive line.

"You wanted to see me?" Schultz asked Milliken.

Milliken sat at the conference table in his office. I sat next to him, computer open.

Schultz remained standing, his arms folded across his chest, clutching the beat-up brown clipboard like a precious object. He'd probably had the thing since his first coaching gig a decade ago.

"As you know, Holt gave Latrell an opportunity to intern in the GM's office. He was selected because . . . well, Latrell, you take it from here."

I tried to make eye contact, but Schultz wasn't having it. I took a deep breath, then started. "Um, I developed a system that predicts the best possible defensive play based on—"

Schultz interrupted. "Is this kid's internship with you or with me?"

Milliken said nothing. It was all on me.

"It's with the GM's office," I answered.

"GM runs the business," Schultz said, his voice gruff. "Coaches run the team."

"I thought you might consider using my system just once," I said, almost whispered.

"How many NFL games have you played? How many have you coached? How many hours of game film have you watched?" If Schultz was on the field, he'd have thrown the clipboard at my feet, I just knew. "Let me answer for you:

zero, zero, zero. You put points on the board and scars on your body, then maybe I'll listen."

"But Frank thought—"

Schultz snorted. "Frank doesn't think."

I wasn't going to let that go. "If Frank and I worked together, if you gave me a chance to call one set of downs—"

"Listen, kid, Frank Foley can't even choose which socks to wear. He's not calling plays for me, and neither are you."

I swallowed hard. "We could contribute if you let us."

Schultz looked hard at Milliken. "Some people earn what they get. Others have it handed to them because someone else wants to feel good about themselves."

Milliken looked up from his phone. "That's enough, Joe."

Schultz and Milliken locked eyes. This wasn't about my system, but something bigger. I'd read that Shultz wanted to be head coach, but Milliken hired media-friendly Allen instead.

"You give me better players, I'll give you better results," Schultz said.

Milliken switched on his smile. "Harmon Holt's name is on your paycheck, and he wants—"

"He wants a winning team," Schulz cut in.

"No, he wants to make money," Milliken said in the tone of a third-grade teacher. "And since it's his money to begin with, he calls the shots. Think about that before this Sunday."

"Are we done?" Schultz asked.

Milliken nodded, but I sensed this wasn't the end of anything, just the beginning.

Schultz left the room while Milliken looked down at the carpet. I knew then what it felt like to be on the fifty-yard line: right in the middle of the action.

TWELVE

September 15 (Saturday)

"Thanks for letting me bring my dirty clothes," I told Roxanne.

"Sure thing," she said.

As she loaded the dryer with the clothes I'd take to Dallas, I gazed at the football shrine that was Franchise Foley's basement. There were photos of great plays and endless trophies in a cabinet. One corner must have had fifty jerseys, hanging from a rack. In another corner stood a life-size cardboard cutout of Frank at the height of his career, smiling, holding his helmet against his hip.

Roxanne finished loading the dryer and joined me in the shrine. "Dad has lots of memories down here." She walked to the jerseys and touched one. "He'll come down here and sit for hours with the lights off."

"Why with the lights off?"

"He says he can hear the crowd that way."

It made me think. Seventeen seasons, every Sunday, playing at the bottom of a Miami or Denver or Buffalo stadium bowl, thousands of eyes on your every move.

Roxanne stood in front of me and grabbed my hands—not in a romantic way, but like she was hanging on for dear life. "Promise me you'll look after Dad in Dallas."

"No problem." I laughed when I said it, but she looked at me hard and serious.

"No, you have to stay with him. That place is huge. He'll get lost in the stadium if you don't."

It was sad, listening to Roxanne talk about her dad like he was two years old, like he was the child and she was the parent. Did that make me a babysitter? "I'll stick with him, Roxanne."

She raised her hand and touched my face. "Thank you," she said. She leaned in. I leaned in soon after, and there, in the shrine to her absentminded father, we kissed.

She drew back. "When you come back, we can spend time together, maybe go to a movie." Her lips felt soft.

I leaned in. Before our second, longer kiss, I said, "I like movies, too."

Frank called from the top of the stairs. "Latrell, MSU just kicked off to Ohio State."

I giggled, and Roxanne did, too. We'd just had our own kickoff of sorts.

* * *

On the plane to Dallas, Frank squeezed his big frame into the small seat. "It was good that Roxanne saw us off at the airport," he said, "I think she likes you."

A wave of nervous energy came over me. "What makes you say that?" I asked.

"You think I didn't see you two kiss before you got to the gate?"

I shrank in my seat. You hear stories about

fathers who don't like guys who date their daughters. Few guys date daughters whose fathers crushed offensive linemen for a living.

I had to say something. "I hope you don't mind, sir."

"Not at all. I just want her happy." He paused. "Roxanne probably told you. Doctors say I have brain damage from all the hits I took. But would I trade losing my car keys for all that football gave me? Probably not."

I wondered what price I'd pay to succeed at something I loved.

"I can always find another set of car keys, but I couldn't get another one of these." He put his hands in front of me to show off the Super Bowl rings. "But it's not about the rings, either." He closed his eyes, tilted his head back, and smiled. "It's the roar of the crowd."

THIRTEEN

September 16 (Sunday) Dallas Cowboys

"They're killing us with junk," I told Milliken as the Cowboys completed another short pass for another first down. I looked at my laptop from the comfort of the suite reserved for visiting GMs. The Cowboys had converted almost every third down in the first half, and the second half started out the same. The Stars defense leaked like a broken boat.

"So, who did you like?" Milliken asked. "The kid from MSU or Ohio State?" Had he written off the season after just a game and a half?

"It depends on what kind of player you want. The guy from MSU has more interceptions and can run the defense. But the Ohio State guy is just a monster, a running back–eating machine."

"Who did Frank like?" As soon as he asked the question, he answered. "Let me guess, the kid from his alma mater who plays like he did?"

"Hands down," I said. Frank trusted my system, but he trusted his gut more.

"We sure could use him now," Milliken shouted over the crowd's roar. Another Dallas TD.

I took a deep breath. "Let me call the next third down situation. I'll make the right call."

Milliken shook his head. "Schultz won't listen to you."

I stood up. "Then make him."

Milliken picked up the phone connected to the coaches on the field. He put his hand over the receiver. "But Joe *might* listen to Frank, out of a sense of loyalty."

I looked at the field. Frank paced on the sidelines, seemingly more agitated than delighted by the roar of the crowd. I looked at Frank, then at my computer, and waited. After the kickoff, the Stars got shut down: an incomplete, a busted sweep, and another quarterback sack. The Stars' punter had more time on the field than the quarterback.

The Cowboys went right to work with two short passes for first downs that got them into scoring position. I added the data and waited. Milliken held the phone in his hand. First down, incomplete. Second down, four yards on a screen. Milliken handed me the phone. It was third and six from the forty, an important down for them and me.

As I looked at Milliken, I spoke to Frank. "This play, call a weak side, CB blitz."

Frank grunted his approval. On the field, I could see him whisper to Schultz. I held my breath. It seemed like the longest snap count in history.

After the snap, the Dallas QB took two steps into the pocket before the Stars' cornerback slammed hard into him, knocking the ball loose.

"Go! Go! Go!" Milliken and I shouted at the same time.

Sims scooped up the fumble, turned on his speed, and never looked back. Not only had I called my first play, I'd scored my first TD.

On the field and on the sidelines, the Stars players celebrated. I watched as Schultz gave Frank a friendly slap on the back. Frank turned in the direction of the suite, looked up, and waved.

FOURTEEN

September 24 (Monday) San Francisco 49ers
"There's nothing like Monday Night Football," Milliken said. Once again, the GM's box was filled with his friends and front-office staff. "In L.A., you get a different crowd on Monday night because the game starts early for the nine o'clock, East Coast start time. New crowd, new revenue."

Milliken rambled on about monetizing opportunities, sounding more like a banker than a football guy. Maybe for him it was all the same.

Although the Stars' offense managed a field

goal in their first possession, they'd need more than that. The 49ers' defense was weak, but their offense was among the strongest in the league. They used a classic run-and-shoot: four receivers, no fullback or tight end. It spread out their offense and was a nightmare to defend. Another wrinkle made them even more deadly: their QB ran like a halfback. They'd won their first two games by thirty. Predictions were they'd win this game by as much. Unless.

At the half, the Stars were down by fourteen as the offense finally clicked. Milliken left the GM box and went to the locker room. Everyone else cleared out with him, leaving me alone. Below me were sixty thousand fans, many thinking that if they cheered loud and long enough, it would make a difference. They acted on faith, not science or facts.

Milliken returned five minutes into the third quarter. After another 49er TD, he took a seat in the recliner. I typed, the crowd roared, but Milliken remained silent until the start of the fourth quarter. "Tell me what play they'll run and what we should do."

I relayed the information, but the phone to the coaches' box stayed untouched. Down after down I told Milliken what we should've done, but on the field, Schultz used old-school D. My computer crushed his clipboard like the 49ers crushed the Stars.

FIFTEEN

September 30 (Sunday) Baltimore Ravens

"It's good to have you home," Mom said. Grandma Estelle, Randall, my aunts, uncles, and various cousins all agreed. "I'm glad the team let you spend the night."

"It's probably so they could save on the cost of a hotel room." Everyone laughed, but I was serious.

"I thought we'd see your name in the paper or on TV." Mom sounded disappointed.

"The stars of the team are the Stars players." I thought one white lie was okay. I saw football as a game of strategy, like chess. Milliken did too, as he pushed around interchangeable pawns. The difference was, I cared if the pawns got crushed.

"We're all so proud of you," Mom said, beaming. "This is your opportunity to do what I couldn't do."

"What's that?"

"Get out of here."

"Why would I want to?" I asked.

Mom shook her head. "You're meant for bigger things than this," she said. She passed around the bowl of scrambled eggs. There was no ham, no bacon, just eggs. It was all she could afford. Back at the Hilton Baltimore, I knew the players were dining on a five-star brunch. As I scooped up another forkful of eggs, they never tasted so good, and my family never felt so strong.

* * *

"Where's Frank?" I asked Earle, the equipment manager, when I entered the locker room. I wanted Frank to meet my family.

"Try the weight room," said Earle.

With the game less than an hour away, I went to the weight room. The lights were off. When I clicked the switch, there was Frank, sitting on a bench in the corner. His eyes were closed, and he was wearing the biggest pair of earphones I'd ever seen.

I tried to get his attention, but he didn't respond. It scared me.

Then Schultz came into the room, kneeled down, and tapped Frank's leg with his clipboard.

Frank pulled his earphones off. Under the earphones, he had earplugs. He pulled those out, too. His ears were open, but his eyes were closed, shut tight as though the faintest amount of light would hurt.

"Getting to be too much for you?" Schultz asked.

"Sometimes I just have to shut it all down," said Frank.

"Are you able to join us on the field today?" Schultz asked. Frank nodded and handed the plugs to Schultz. Schultz looked puzzled. "Why are you giving these to me?"

"Might as well make it official. You don't listen anyway."

"Frank, once the game starts, it's my defense. You had a good call during the Cowboys game, but—"

"It wasn't mine, it was his." Frank pointed at me. His hand shook just like my knees.

"We're oh and three on the season. You really want to go oh and four?" Frank asked.

Schultz said nothing.

Frank stood up and put his arm on my shoulder.

I took the opportunity to speak. "The Ravens offense has weaknesses we can exploit. The left side of their line is—"

Schultz cut me off. "I watch the game films, too. Tell me something I don't know."

I took my cue. "In their first three games, they—" I started. I went on for a good two minutes, giving him the hard sell on everything I knew to help us win.

Schultz thought for a moment, then spoke. "I'm the defensive coordinator, not you, kid. And not Frank," he said, brow furrowed.

"Frank and I have the system. I ran the numbers. He watched the film. We can do this."

Frank jumped in. "He's right, Joe. The kid's system works."

I didn't like it when Schultz called me a kid, but coming from Frank, it was okay. We were partners, trying to bring sight to the sightless.

Schultz paused. "I know you have problems, Frank," he said.

"My problem is the guy I played beside for almost a decade doesn't trust my football judgment," Frank said. "Trust us, Joe."

Schultz sighed.

"You're winless," I said. "You have nothing to lose."

Another sigh, only bigger, meaner. "Okay," Schultz said with a scowl on his face, "but I have two conditions."

"Name 'em," Frank said as he sat back down.

"We keep it between us. No one on the team and no one in the media learns about this, got it? I can't have my defense becoming some sideshow."

"Milliken has to know." Frank put his hand out. Schultz dropped the earplugs in his palm.

"Between the four of us, then," Schultz said. "But if things start to go wrong, I take over."

"Fine." Frank closed his eyes and put the plugs back in his ears.

"And another thing—" Schultz started.

Frank cut him off. "Here's my condition. Turn the lights off on your way out. Come get me when it's game time."

SIXTEEN

October 1 (Monday)

Every phone in the Stars' front office rang all morning except mine. The ancient beige phone in the tiny conference room Milliken had arranged to be my "office" was silent. And when I tried to get in to see Milliken about next week's game or another assignment, I was told he was too busy.

I killed time by loading data from yesterday's victory over the Ravens into my model. Next week's team, the Lions, was also coming off a big victory, so interest in the game was huge.

After I loaded the data, I ran my model. If

Schultz, through Frank, used my defense like he had against the Ravens, we'd destroy the Lions. They might beat us on first down, which was hardest to predict, but we'd shut them down on second and third. For the first time, *we* felt like the right word. I no longer felt like an outsider.

When the phone finally did ring, I jumped. It wasn't Milliken. It was Kevin, my roommate. "Congrats on the big win," he said.

"Thanks," I said with a new pride in my voice. "You know I lived it."

"What do you mean?" asked Kevin.

After he promised not to tell a soul, I'd told him everything—about the confrontation in the weight room, about Frank and I calling the defensive plays. Like me, he was at his internship. Like him, I was finally making a real contribution.

"The first opportunity was to get the internship, but the second was to succeed," I said. "It's only one game, but I proved to them my system works. Data matters."

"Well, if you ever get tired of grown men bashing each other's brains in, we could use your smarts over here. We're making lighter, tougher armor for soldiers."

"I don't think that's going to happen, because as we keep winning, they'll show loyalty to me and tell people what I—"

Kevin laughed, too loud for something that wasn't meant as a joke. "Seriously?"

"Seriously what?"

Another bolt of lightning laughter from him; another jolt of thunder anger from me.

"Latrell, do you seriously think they're going to let anyone know that a seventeen-year-old kid is secretly running the defense? We're interns. We're unpaid and invisible, especially you."

"I'm sure Milliken will—" But then I stopped in midsentence. Was I exiled from Milliken's office because I'd succeeded?

I flipped on the TV that displayed four cameras from around the stadium. In one corner of the screen, Allen sat with reporters huddled all around. Frank was nowhere in sight.

Kevin and I talked until the call came from Milliken.

I hustled into his office. He sat behind his desk, smoking a cigar. I coughed.

"You wanted to see me?"

On the wall of his office were five TVs: three set to local stations, one to Fox, the other to ESPN. He didn't say a word to me, but on the TVs his voice boomed like a conquering general's. I stood still, almost at attention, like a soldier. A loyal, lowly foot soldier. A pawn.

He stared at the TVs, smoked, smiled like he meant it, and listened to his own voice.

Finally, I spoke. "I have the matchups for Sunday's game."

"Good." He flashed that fake smile, but the angry frown on my face was real.

"It's not fair," I mumbled as I pointed at his image on the TV screens, taking credit for the Stars' win.

"You're right, Latrell. It's not fair. But we can't have some math-whiz-kid sideshow story. It'd be a distraction." He sucked smoke into his lungs, held it for a moment, then said, "It's not what's best for Latrell. It's what's best for the team."

SEVENTEEN

October 2 (Tuesday)

Roxanne placed the cake on the table. It was a three-layer cake made from scratch. The top layers leaned like a short, wide tower about to fall.

"A lopsided cake for a lopsided victory," laughed Frank.

"Now, Dad, you know what happens when you make fun of the cook?" asked Roxanne.

Frank looked at me and laughed that big, booming laugh of his. "You starve!"

"That's right," said Roxanne. "Now, eat up. It's red velvet. Your favorite."

Frank handed me the knife. "You do the honors, Latrell. It was your victory more than anyone else's."

I was glad my system got recognition, if only from Frank. My system had stopped the Raven's offense, just as I knew it would. It placed their defense on the field too much, and the Stars' offense took advantage. I slid the knife into the pink frosting. "Thanks for the honors. I just wish you and I got credit for it."

"That's not gonna happen, son," he said.

I made a mental note. It was the first time he'd called me "son." I liked it.

"When a team wins, all eyes should be on the players," Frank said. "But in L.A., the only stars are the ones in suits. Allen's crap as a coach, except when he listens to his coordinators."

"We'll take the Lions on Sunday. With back-to-back wins, folks will catch on."

Frank took a bite of cake. "You really think they care?"

"They gotta care some," I said. After I said it, I doubted myself. "Don't they?"

Frank dug out another forkful of cake.

"When I went to Milliken after the doctor told me about my head injury, they first told me I couldn't blame it on football. Then they told me I should have played smarter on the field and not hit so much."

I looked over at Roxanne. She pushed the cake with her fork, but she wasn't eating. "Did you know that?" I asked.

"I do now," she said. "All Dad wanted was to be better than anyone else on the field." She looked up at me. "And look where it got him."

Frank went for another slice of cake as the wheels in my mind turned. I'd help Schultz on Sunday, give him the best defensive calls, and we'd crush the Lions' offense.

It dawned on me then. The system that brought me here—my numbers, charts, percentages—could spell success, just like it did in last week. But in the process, I'd be the one making more players like Frank. Football was a head-crunching machine, and I'd become a cog.

EIGHTEEN

October* 7 *(Sunday) Detroit Lions

Stars Stadium was half-full when players from both teams came out for warm-ups. Even at half capacity, the noise was deafening.

Frank surveyed the crowd, a huge grin on his face.

"This is what you were talking about, right? The roar of the crowd?" I asked.

"When you do something that makes sixty thousand people cheer, there's nothing like it."

"Well, I'm hoping for another win today."

Frank focused on the field. He kicked the

dirt. "Schultz doesn't trust you or me."

"But the Lions' offense is so predictable. If he'll just listen to me—"

"He's in a tough spot. He wants to win, but he's got his pride," said Frank. "Once you lose that, you've lost it all."

* * *

The second half was pure good news. The Stars' defense shut down the Lions' attack in all but two plays. In the first play, Schultz called an outside linebacker blitz against the model's recommendation. The Lions saw it coming, called an audible, and a short, five-yard flare led to a seventy-five-yard sprint to the end zone. Then the Lions made a bizarre call in a situation that called for a handoff to the fullback, but they faked it and threw a long pass for a second TD. Trouble was, my model only predicted logical play-calling, but humans—even football coaches and players—were not always logical.

The Lions were scoreless in the second half. The Stars' D kept them to under a hundred yards combined. The offense did enough to give the defense a lead to hold. As the last seconds ticked down, the crowd roared.

"Congratulations, Latrell. You succeeded at this assignment," Milliken said.

I expected a handshake but got a hard slap on the back instead.

NINETEEN

October 12 (Friday)

"Latrell, the Stars are like a family, and families sometimes need to keep things secret," Milliken said as I followed him into a large conference room. Schultz and two white guys in suits sat at the table.

Milliken continued. "We're going to tell some people in the office about your system, but nobody outside can know. I mean, if another team found out, they'd try to take you away from us, and we'd lose our edge. And in football, you need every edge you can get."

Schultz added, "Or worse, you could become a distraction to the players. Who knows what would happen if they found out a kid was calling the plays?"

"I understand. I just want the chance to prove myself," I said.

"You will." Milliken pointed at the two guys in suits. "So, let me introduce you to Bill Palmer, our head stat guy, and Steve Snider, in charge of IT."

I shook their hands.

"Now, all of your data is on a laptop—" Milliken started.

"That's not secure or fast enough," Snider interrupted.

"I know you've got good data, but I have access to more of it," said Palmer.

"So during the game, you'll relay the defensive setup call—" Milliken said.

It was Schultz's turn to interrupt. "You mean his *suggested* call."

Milliken flashed the fake smile. "You, Bill, and Steve will be a team. I want them to work with you. In a sense, they'll be *your* interns.

Teach them the ins and outs of your system. When the season's over, we'll see that you get credit."

"I don't know if I can wait four more months," I said.

"Four months?" Snider asked.

I held the room's attention like I owned it. "Right, four months," I said. "The Super Bowl isn't until February."

TWENTY

October 14 (Sunday) Denver Broncos

"Congratulations, Latrell!" Milliken shouted as the final seconds ticked off the clock. Another Stars victory and another defensive shutout. Although the Broncos had scored two touchdowns—one a punt return and another on a fumble—the only time they'd mounted sustained drives was when Schultz ignored my system.

"I have to admit, I didn't believe it, but down after down, you predicted right," Palmer said. In reviewing my model before the game, he'd expressed his doubt. But unlike Schultz, who was old-school, Palmer believed in stats.

"I have to get to the press room for interviews, but before I do—" Milliken took out his wallet and handed me five twenty-dollar bills. "You have a girlfriend, Latrell?"

I blushed, nodded, looked away, but said nothing.

"Why don't you take her out tonight and—" He stopped talking when something on TV grabbed his attention. He grabbed the remote, unmuted the TV, and we all watched. The sideline reporter had his mic in front of Frank, who smiled into the camera.

"As linebacker coach, your guys made some key plays today, Frank. Tell us—"

"Get him off the TV, now!" Milliken shouted into his phone. As loud as he yelled, I'm sure they could've heard him all the way down on the field. "Do it now, or you're fired!"

I stared at the screen. I remembered Frank's interviews back when he was a player. I thought he earned the nickname "Franchise" because he had such command on the field. But now his expression was almost like that of a child. Frank talked, but wasn't making a lot of sense.

"Frank," the interviewer insisted, "I think what you're saying—"

Schultz entered the screen, wrapped his arm around Frank, and whispered something.

"Frank's not feeling well today," Schultz then told the interviewer. "I'll take questions in the press room."

I turned back to say something to Milliken, but his chair was empty.

* * *

After he reached the press room, Milliken called to tell me not to leave and to continue to explain my system to Palmer and Snider. I went over the data with them as best as I could as Milliken, Allen, and even Smackdown Schultz beamed for the cameras on the TV behind us. After an hour, as a hundred dollars burned a hole in my pocket and thoughts of Roxanne smoked in my brain, Milliken returned. He took one step into the room and motioned for Palmer and Snider to join him. The three of them huddled briefly, then Milliken sat with me at the table as Palmer and Snider closed the door behind them.

"So, you wanted an internship in the GM's office? You thought you'd get to meet players, deal with agents, all that fun, exciting stuff, right?" Milliken asked.

Before I could answer, he started again. "This is a hard game, and I'm not talking about how hard it is on the field. Players take their hits, but what I do up here hurts just as much."

"I don't understand—"

"Maybe a computer can call plays, but winning teams need leadership on the field and from this room."

I needed more information. "What are you trying to say?"

He took a seat in the big chair that overlooked the field. He poured another drink and lit a victory cigar.

"You're going to learn leadership through action." Milliken sipped his drink and blew out smoke. "Before our next game, I need you to help me fire Frank."

My jaw dropped.

Milliken continued, "I know you've gotten friendly with his daughter."

I started to talk but he cut me off.

"Just listen. The way I figure, if you can convince her to tell her dad he's got to quit for his health, she'll listen. We can make this whole thing go away without any damage to the organization. Without any embarrassment."

"But Mr. Milliken I can't—"

"Enough. You can, Latrell. If you've proved anything in the last few weeks, you've proved you can be very persuasive. Get this done, and you'll find my gratitude is well worth having."

TWENTY-ONE

October 17 (Wednesday)

As we searched for a parking space, the clunker gave off a loud *boom* that echoed off the buildings on campus. I ducked in the seat from embarrassment while Frank pumped his fist in the air. "We're here!" he shouted. That's what I liked best about Frank. He kept it real, didn't mask the truth or cover things up.

And while Milliken was making me choose between the Stars and the Foleys, I didn't need an algorithm to know what was best for me.

The class assignment for the day was to bring

someone from where we worked to speak to the class. I chose the one person I respected most.

Roxanne and I entered the class first. Everyone went silent when they saw Roxanne. Then came Frank. With shoulders that went on forever, he turned sideways to get through the door. I think he was pretty proud of the fact, too. He looked back at the doorway, laughed, then turned to class, stomped his big foot forward, and growled. It was classic Frank. If folks only knew what a teddy bear he truly was.

Mr. Casey jumped up from his desk. "Well, Latrell, I see you brought your internship guests for the day." He seemed impressed and maybe little afraid.

"This is Franchise Foley," I said, "and this is his daughter, Roxanne. She's here to watch, really. Frank's my guest."

When I said Frank's name, a couple of guys clapped. I knew that filled Frank's heart.

Roxanne took a seat in the back of the room, but finding a seat for Frank was another matter. He tried one of the classroom chairs but was just too big for it. That's when Mr. Casey took the seat from behind his desk and wheeled it over. "Here, take mine."

With Frank seated in front of the class, I spoke. "Of course, you all know my internship has been with the L.A. Stars." I thought for a moment. "First and foremost, the Stars are a business, so I don't want you to think it's been all glamorous and whatnot. In fact, the most I've learned about the game of football, I learned from this man here."

Frank leaned forward and held his hand up, showing everyone his Super Bowl rings. "You know how hard you have to work to get one of these?" he asked. "Daily workouts. Endless film sessions. Living in the weight room. I've played football for so long, I can't even remember it all. But there's a reason for that."

Frank paused. I looked at Roxanne. She sat at a desk, her chin in her palm.

"You see, I can't remember much at all anymore," Frank confessed in a hushed tone.

I looked at the students. They seemed puzzled.

He took a deep breath that sliced the silence. "Anyone ever heard of a concussion?"

Most every student nodded.

"I've had so many concussions, I've taken so many hits, the doctors say my brain has these small holes in it." Frank held up his big hands and formed circles with his fingers. "They told me the name of the disease, but I can't even remember that!" He laughed aloud.

I'd had no idea Frank was going to say this. I looked over at Mr. Casey. He looked as puzzled as I did.

Frank leaned in toward the students like he'd done against the offensive line for seventeen years. "If you love football, just remember me. You want to keep playing? Just know there are risks. But I guess that's true of whatever you do. Follow your dreams, make smart choices, and don't give up the best part of yourself, because if you do—"

The room grew silent for the longest time. I looked at Roxanne. She had pulled a tissue from her purse and was wiping her eyes. Frank also looked at his daughter. "If you do, those dreams might turn into nightmares for the people you love."

I put my hand on Frank's shoulder. "Thank you, Frank." I started to clap. Then, the teacher clapped, and the clapping grew louder as other students joined in. Then, everyone stood, and the clapping grew even louder. Once again, Frank had earned the respect and the roar of the crowd.

TWENTY-TWO

October 17 (Wednesday p.m.)

"Latrell, I'm very disappointed." Milliken sat at his desk. I stood in front of him. I guess this was what an old-fashioned firing squad was like, except I hadn't been blindfolded first. "Not only did you not help with Frank like I told you to, but taking him to class was inappropriate. Taking him to class so he could talk publicly about his health problems was insane."

"Why did you ask me to help fire him?"

Milliken scowled. "I didn't *ask* you, I told you. Failing to do so is insubordination, which is a fireable offense. I might have let it slide, but to take him to class and subject him to the humiliation—"

"He wasn't humiliated," I said defiantly. "He wanted to do it. He wanted to show—"

"Look, football gives and takes. He knew the risks, but he was rewarded all the same."

I thought about Holt's limo and Milliken's BMW. I thought about Frank's clunker.

"No," I said. "You and guys like Holt got the rewards, Frank took all the risk."

"Well, you took a risk, Latrell, and now you face the consequences," he said. "Clean out your desk. I'll tell Mr. Holt your services are no longer needed."

"I did what I thought was right."

"It's a shame, Latrell. We're on a roll now, a real winning streak."

"Thanks to my system."

He flashed the smile. "No, *our* system. We own it now."

I turned on my heel and never looked back as I spoke under my breath. "But you don't own me."

"They fired me." I called Uncle Randall the moment after I cleaned out my desk, but not before one final piece of business.

"I'm sorry, Latrell."

"Well, now it means I can pass along inside information. This Sunday, bet a lot."

"Another shutout?" Randall asked. He was almost panting on the phone.

"I can't speak for the offense, but I wouldn't bet on the Stars' defense or the integrity of its data." I laughed at the word *integrity*. I then hit the enter button, transferring data from my laptop into the Stars' cloud, a cloud now filled not with a silver lining, but with corrupt facts. Just as I'd thought, Milliken hadn't told anyone in IT to suspend my passwords.

"Last week, my bookie thought I was crazy to bet on the Stars. But I'm heading out soon to pay off my car, then to mail you a cool percent of what I made."

"You don't need to do that," I said. I shouldn't be rewarded for my sabotage.

"Call it recognition for a job well done," said

Randall. "No one else gave you credit, so it's up to me."

* * *

Roxanne picked me up to bring me to the house. When I stepped inside, Frank greeted me with a handshake. "Hey, son, I heard what Milliken did. I guess Roxanne told you I got canned, too."

I stood with my hands in my pockets, as there was little else to do.

"Come into the living room. I have something for you."

I sat next to Roxanne on the couch.

"What's going on?" I asked.

"I don't know," she said after her father left the room. "But losing his job may be a blessing in disguise. The further we are from football the better, as far as I'm concerned."

Frank returned with a trophy in his hand. "This was for Super Bowl MVP." He handed it to me.

It felt heavy, but no heavier than the price he'd paid, earning it. I looked at it, then handed it back to him, but he wouldn't take it.

"It's yours. I insist," he said.

"But I—I can't take this, Frank."

"You gave so much to me and Roxanne, I want to give you something in return. Besides, you earned it."

I pulled the trophy closer and pictured how it would look in my room in DC.

Frank then took one of his jerseys from the back of his chair and handed it to me.

"Frank, this is just—" I reached over and hugged him. It was a big moment for me. "Maybe when I get back to DC, the Redskins or the Ravens will pick me up."

Frank smiled. "You'll do well wherever you go. I just know."

"But I guess a lot depends on two things," I said, feeling humbled.

"What are those?"

"Someone like Holt to give me an opportunity," I talked fast so I wouldn't cry. "And somebody like you to believe in me."

TWENTY-THREE

Dear Mr. Holt:

I'll always be grateful for the opportunity you gave me.

I'm sorry I couldn't finish my internship—but not as sorry as I'd be if I'd finished it on Milliken's terms. You said this was an opportunity to prove myself. I don't know if I proved myself to you, but I know I proved myself to the one who matters most: me.

Sincerely,
Latrell

ABOUT THE AUTHORS

Patrick Jones is the author of six novels for teens, most recently the supernatural tome *The Tear Collector.* A former librarian for teenagers, Jones received lifetime achievement awards from the American Library Association and the Catholic Library Association in 2006. While he lives in Minneapolis, he still considers Flint, Michigan, his hometown. He can be found on the web at www .connectingya.com and on front of his television on Monday nights watching wrestling.

A former magazine editor, Brent Chartier is author of *Iceland: A Hockey Novel* and *Sandy's Beautiful Flowers.* His interest in traumatic brain injury is a result of his work with the Center for Neurological Studies, Dearborn, MI. He lives in Chesterfield, MI.